CW00797092

THE MIND GAMES

The Mind Games

A Thriller of Psychological Warfare

FINNEGAN JONES

RWG Publishing

Contents

Contents ~ vii

Chapter 1

Chapter 1: "The Puppet Master's Prelude"

The city was enshrouded in a dense fog, an atmospheric prelude to the chaos about to unfold. Detective Lucas Black stared out of his office window, the city lights muted by the mist. His mind, though weary, was on high alert as he awaited news on the latest case—a string of mysterious disappearances that had gripped the metropolis.

The Puppet Master, as the media had labeled the elusive perpetrator, seemed to possess an uncanny ability to control minds, leaving no trace of evidence behind. The victims vanished without a trace, their minds seemingly wiped clean.

Lucas shuffled through the scattered notes on his desk, each one a testament to his frustration and determination to crack the case. The clock on the wall ticked away, a constant reminder of time slipping through his fingers.

The phone rang, shattering the silence of the room. It was his partner, Detective Sarah Martinez, her voice laden with urgency. "Lucas, I've got something. Meet me at the abandoned warehouse on East End Avenue. I think I've found a lead."

Without hesitation, Lucas grabbed his coat and bolted out of the office, the fog wrapping around him like a sinister cloak. The warehouse loomed ahead, a dilapidated structure standing as a relic of the city's forgotten past.

Sarah stood near the entrance, a flashlight in hand, her eyes fixed on the eerie shadows dancing within. As Lucas approached, she gestured towards a set of footprints leading deeper into the warehouse, disappearing into the darkness.

Together, they ventured into the labyrinthine corridors, their footsteps echoing against the desolate walls. The air was thick with an unsettling stillness, broken only by the distant sound of machinery humming faintly.

They stumbled upon a small room concealed behind a rusted door. Inside, a makeshift laboratory lay in disarray —computers flickered with fragmented codes, vials of unknown substances cluttered the tables, and intricate diagrams adorned the walls, hinting at a mind consumed by obsession.

Sarah pointed at a journal lying open on the table, its pages filled with cryptic writings and sketches of brain patterns. "This could be it," she said, her voice hushed with a mix of anticipation and unease.

Lucas flipped through the journal, piecing together fragmented entries that hinted at experiments in mind manipulation and control. The Puppet Master's modus operandi was slowly unraveling before their eyes.

As they continued their search, a sudden noise reverberated through the warehouse—a chilling laughter that seemed to echo from the very walls. Adrenaline surged through their veins as they exchanged wary glances, their senses heightened.

The laughter intensified, growing louder and more unnerving. Suddenly, the warehouse plunged into darkness, engulfing them in a suffocating blackness.

In the pitch-black abyss, a voice taunted them, weaving through the shadows like a sinister melody. "You think you can unravel my game? How amusing." The voice resonated with a haunting certainty, sending shivers down their spines.

Desperate to escape the oppressive darkness, Lucas and Sarah fumbled for their flashlights. As the beams cut through the obsidian veil, they found themselves alone in the abandoned warehouse, the laughter fading into an eerie silence.

With their nerves on edge, they made a swift exit, haunted by the ominous presence that lingered in the air. The Puppet Master's prelude had set the stage for a chilling cat-and-mouse game, leaving Lucas and Sarah with more questions than answers.

Chapter 2

Chapter 2: "Echoes of Deception"

The morning sun peeked through the blinds of Lucas Black's apartment, casting warm rays across the room. He sat at his cluttered dining table, the remnants of a sleepless night evident in the dark circles beneath his eyes. The events of the previous day lingered in his mind like an unresolved puzzle, each piece a haunting echo of deception.

His phone buzzed, interrupting the silence. It was Sarah. "Lucas, we need to meet. There's something you have to see."

Without a word, Lucas grabbed his keys and hurried out, the echo of Sarah's urgency ringing in his ears. The drive to their rendezvous point felt endless, the cityscape passing by in a blur.

Sarah awaited him near the crime scene of the latest disappearance. As Lucas approached, he was greeted by a sense of foreboding that clung to the air like a palpable entity.

Sarah pointed to a series of cryptic symbols etched into the wall of the alleyway—a language unfamiliar, yet hauntingly familiar. "This wasn't here yesterday," she said, her voice tinged with unease.

Lucas examined the symbols, a shiver running down his spine. They resembled patterns he had seen in the journal from the warehouse—an unsettling connection that sent a chill through his veins.

As they canvassed the area for clues, a commotion drew their attention to a nearby building. A woman, disoriented and visibly shaken, stumbled out, her eyes vacant, as if robbed of their soul.

Rushing to her aid, Lucas and Sarah attempted to calm her, but she mumbled incoherently, her gaze fixated on some invisible horror that haunted her mind.

"Echoes," she muttered, her voice trembling. "Deceptive echoes in my head, pulling me into their lies."

Her cryptic words only deepened the mystery. Lucas scribbled down her words in his notebook, each syllable a potential clue in the labyrinth of the Puppet Master's mind games.

The woman's distress mirrored the pattern of the previous disappearances—a disturbing repetition that sent a shudder through Lucas. It was as if the echoes of deception were reverberating through the city, ensnaring unsuspecting victims in their web of manipulation.

As they escorted the woman to safety, Lucas's mind raced with questions. How were these symbols connected to the disappearances? What did the echoes signify? And who was orchestrating this sinister symphony of deception?

Back at the precinct, Lucas delved into the database, scouring through records of similar incidents, seeking a pattern that could offer a glimmer of understanding. Sarah paced the room, her frustration mirroring his own.

Hours passed in relentless pursuit of answers, but the threads they sought remained elusive, teasingly out of reach. The echo of the woman's words lingered in Lucas's mind, a cryptic riddle begging to be deciphered.

As the night descended upon the city once more, Lucas and Sarah found themselves at a crossroads, caught in the haunting echoes of deception that seemed to permeate every corner of their investigation. The Puppet Master's game was far from over, leaving them entangled in a maze of uncertainty and deceit.

Chapter 3

Chapter 3: "A Mind's Battlefield"

In the aftermath of the unsettling events, Lucas Black found himself consumed by the enigmatic puzzle that was the Puppet Master's mind games. Nightmares haunted his sleep, visions of distorted symbols and echoing whispers entangled in a relentless battle within his own mind.

The morning arrived, casting a feeble attempt at light through the curtains of his apartment. Lucas, weary from restless thoughts, trudged to the precinct, his mind a battlefield of conflicting theories and unanswered questions.

Sarah awaited him, her expression a mirror of his own inner turmoil. "Lucas, I've been digging into the history of the symbols we found. They trace back to an ancient text— one associated with the manipulation of consciousness and perception."

Her revelation sparked a glimmer of hope amidst the chaos. Could these symbols hold the key to unraveling the Puppet Master's sinister plot?

Together, they pored over dusty tomes and obscure archives, immersing themselves in the arcane knowledge of mind control and psychological warfare. The deeper they delved, the more the lines between reality and illusion blurred, plunging them into the heart of a mind's battlefield.

The ancient text spoke of a power beyond comprehension—a force that could shape thoughts, bend wills, and distort reality itself. The Puppet Master seemed to be wielding this forbidden knowledge with chilling expertise.

As dusk descended, a breakthrough emerged from the depths of their research—an obscure reference to a clandestine group rumored to possess the secrets of mental manipulation. The Society of Phantasmic Cognition—a name whispered in hushed tones, shrouded in mystery and intrigue.

Lucas and Sarah exchanged a knowing glance. The Puppet Master's machinations seemed intricately tied to this elusive society, an underground network lurking in the shadows, orchestrating a clandestine war on the battlefield of the mind.

With a newfound determination, they set out to trace the footsteps of this clandestine group, their investigation leading them to the underbelly of the city—a realm where truth danced with deception, and reality was a fragile construct.

Their pursuit led them to an abandoned library, rumored to house esoteric knowledge hidden from the world. Dust-covered shelves adorned with ancient tomes greeted their arrival, the air thick with the scent of forgotten wisdom.

As they combed through the neglected archives, a hidden compartment revealed itself, unveiling a trove of

THE MIND GAMES ~ 9

manuscripts adorned with the same cryptic symbols. The manuscripts detailed rituals, experiments, and the insidious power wielded by the Society of Phantasmic Cognition—a power that transcended the boundaries of the known world.

The revelation sent a chill down Lucas's spine. The Puppet Master's motives were becoming clearer, a sinister plot woven into the fabric of ancient knowledge and clandestine societies.

With each page turned, the mind's battlefield expanded, blurring the lines between what was real and what was an illusion. Lucas and Sarah stood at the precipice of a revelation that could unravel the very fabric of their reality—a truth that threatened to consume them in its relentless pursuit.

Chapter 4

Chapter 4: "Threads of Manipulation"

In the dimly lit confines of Lucas Black's apartment, the weight of the Puppet Master's schemes bore down upon him. The haunting revelations from their investigation into the Society of Phantasmic Cognition left Lucas grappling with a sense of unease that seemed to weave itself into the very fabric of his existence.

As night fell, Lucas found himself poring over the notes scattered across his coffee table, each piece of information a thread in the intricate tapestry of manipulation spun by their elusive adversary.

Sarah arrived, her face etched with determination. "Lucas, I've managed to track down a former member of the society. He might have answers."

Without hesitation, they set out to meet this informant, navigating through labyrinthine alleys and obscure locations—each step a tug on the threads of manipulation guiding them closer to the truth.

They arrived at a secluded apartment, its dimly lit interior casting elongated shadows across the walls. The former member, a man weathered by time and secrets, greeted them with a haunted expression.

"I left that life behind," he murmured, his voice laden with regret. "But I can't ignore what I know."

As they settled in, the informant shared fragments of his past—a life entangled with the clandestine workings of the society, where the threads of manipulation were woven with a finesse that bordered on the supernatural.

He spoke of clandestine meetings in the shadows, where minds were sculpted and realities bent to the whims of those who wielded this forbidden knowledge. The Puppet Master, a name whispered with reverence and fear, was said to possess a mastery that surpassed even the most adept members of the society.

The informant's words painted a chilling picture of manipulation—of threads woven with precision, entangling unsuspecting victims in a web of control, their thoughts mere puppets in the hands of a malevolent puppeteer.

As the night wore on, a knock at the door shattered the tense silence. A shadowy figure loomed in the doorway, their presence a menacing echo of the Puppet Master's reach.

The informant's expression twisted in fear. "They've found me," he gasped, a tremor in his voice.

In a swift motion, the figure lunged forward, wielding a power that seemed to warp reality itself. The room trembled as unseen forces clashed, a manifestation of the threads of manipulation converging in a chaotic dance.

Lucas and Sarah sprang into action, their instincts honed by months of pursuing the elusive Puppet Master. In the ensuing struggle, the informant managed to slip away, leaving behind a whirlwind of confusion and shattered remnants of the truth.

The shadowy figure, thwarted by their resistance, vanished into the night, leaving Lucas and Sarah shaken but determined to untangle the threads that bound their investigation.

As they regrouped in the aftermath of the encounter, Lucas realized they were treading on precarious ground—a battlefield where the Puppet Master's threads of manipulation held sway, entwining them in a perilous game with consequences that reached far beyond their understanding.

Chapter 5

Chapter 5: "The Web of Intrigue"

In the wake of the tumultuous encounter at the informant's apartment, Lucas Black and Sarah Martinez found themselves entangled in a labyrinth of uncertainty. The Puppet Master's elusive maneuvers had woven a dense web of intrigue, ensnaring their investigation in a tangle of deceit and danger.

Back at the precinct, they sifted through the fragments of the informant's revelations, piecing together the threads of information that hinted at the Puppet Master's insidious plot. The Society of Phantasmic Cognition, a clandestine organization shrouded in secrecy, appeared to serve as the Puppet Master's conduit to power.

Lucas paced the dimly lit room, his mind a whirlwind of conjectures and fragmented truths. Sarah poured over case files, her brow furrowed in concentration as she attempted to decipher the cryptic patterns in the Puppet Master's machinations.

The web of intrigue expanded, each strand connecting to another in a complex tapestry of manipulation and subterfuge. Every lead they pursued seemed to vanish into the ether, leaving behind only elusive traces of the Puppet Master's presence.

In a desperate attempt to untangle the web, Lucas delved into the city's underbelly, seeking whispers and rumors that might lead them closer to the truth. Dark alleyways and clandestine meeting spots became their haunting grounds, each encounter a potential clue in their quest to unravel the enigma.

Their investigation led them to an abandoned building at the edge of the city—a derelict structure whispered to house the remnants of the society's clandestine gatherings. As they cautiously navigated the decrepit corridors, the air thickened with an oppressive silence, amplifying the sense of foreboding that lingered in the shadows.

They stumbled upon a hidden chamber adorned with eerie symbols and arcane markings—a grim reminder of the society's clandestine rituals. Dust-covered manuscripts and artifacts lay scattered, remnants of a world veiled in secrecy and ancient knowledge.

Among the scattered relics, they discovered a tome—a chronicle of the society's history, its pages recounting tales of mind manipulation and the Puppet Master's ascendance within their ranks. The secrets within the tome unveiled a history steeped in darkness, unveiling the true extent of the Puppet Master's prowess in weaving his intricate web of intrigue.

As they pored over the ancient texts, a realization struck Lucas—a revelation hidden within the cryptic passages hinted at an upcoming convergence, a pivotal moment when the Puppet Master's plans would reach their apex.

The looming convergence became a focal point in their investigation—a nexus where the threads of manipulation intertwined, guiding them towards an impending climax that threatened to shatter the fragile equilibrium between reality and illusion.

With the weight of this revelation pressing upon them, Lucas and Sarah stood on the precipice of a revelation that promised to unravel the intricacies of the Puppet Master's enigmatic web of intrigue. The looming convergence became a beacon of hope in their relentless pursuit of truth amidst the shadows of uncertainty.

Chapter 6

Chapter 6: "Illusions Unraveled"

In the wake of their discoveries surrounding the impending convergence, Lucas Black and Sarah Martinez found themselves in a relentless pursuit to decipher the Puppet Master's intricate illusions. The looming convergence stood as a linchpin in their investigation—a moment where the veil of deception threatened to unravel, exposing the true machinations of their elusive adversary.

Their quest for truth led them through a maze of deception, navigating through a city shrouded in uncertainty and paranoia. Lucas poured over ancient texts and esoteric knowledge, seeking clues that could unveil the illusions woven by the Puppet Master's adept manipulation.

Sarah delved into the digital realm, tracing digital footprints and encrypted messages that hinted at the Puppet Master's cryptic designs. The illusions created by their adversary seemed to ripple through every facet of their investigation, obscuring reality with a veil of uncertainty.

Their pursuit led them to a dilapidated theater nestled in the heart of the city—a forgotten relic from a bygone era. The grandeur of its architecture stood in stark contrast to the decay that had befallen its halls, echoing the fading glamour of a forgotten past.

Within the abandoned theater's confines, the duo discovered remnants of the Puppet Master's presence—an intricately crafted stage adorned with arcane symbols and enigmatic apparatus. The theater, once a bastion of entertainment, now served as a haunting canvas for the Puppet Master's illusions.

As they explored the eerie corridors and forgotten wings of the theater, illusions manifested before their eyes—whispers that seemed to dance on the edge of reality, mirages that toyed with their perceptions.

In the heart of the theater, they stumbled upon a hidden chamber—a sanctum where the Puppet Master's illusions reached their zenith. A room adorned with mirrors, each one a gateway to a kaleidoscope of distorted realities. The air crackled with a surreal energy, a testament to the Puppet Master's mastery in crafting illusions that transcended the boundaries of the mind.

Lucas and Sarah stood amidst the mirrors, the reflections warping and twisting with each passing moment. The boundaries between what was real and what was illusion blurred, leaving them teetering on the precipice of uncertainty.

With a surge of determination, Lucas reached out, shattering the closest mirror with a resounding crash. The illusion fractured, revealing the truth hidden behind the facades meticulously crafted by the Puppet Master.

As the shards fell to the ground, the illusory realm collapsed around them, dispelling the fabricated realities that had clouded their minds. The theater echoed with the shattering of illusions, leaving behind a palpable silence that hung in the air—a stark contrast to the chaos that had consumed the moment before.

In the aftermath, Lucas and Sarah emerged from the shattered illusions, their resolve strengthened by the revelation. The Puppet Master's elaborate illusions had unraveled, revealing a glimpse of the true tapestry of manipulation woven by their adversary.

With newfound clarity, they stood ready to confront the looming convergence—a pivotal moment where the tangled threads of deception and truth would converge, setting the stage for the ultimate showdown in their relentless battle against the Puppet Master's illusions.

Chapter 7

Chapter 7: "Shadows of Doubt"

In the aftermath of the shattered illusions within the abandoned theater, Lucas Black and Sarah Martinez found themselves shrouded in shadows of doubt. The revelations of the Puppet Master's illusions had shaken the foundation of their investigation, leaving behind lingering uncertainties that loomed like ominous specters.

As they regrouped in Lucas's apartment, the weight of the recent events bore down upon them. The shattered mirrors, once gateways to illusory realms, now reflected a fractured reality—a reality fraught with uncertainty and lingering questions.

Their pursuit of the truth seemed mired in a nebulous haze, the tendrils of doubt creeping into the very fabric of their understanding. Lucas paced the room, his mind wrestling with the implications of the illusions they had encountered.

"Sarah, what if everything we've seen is just another layer of the Puppet Master's manipulation?" Lucas's voice was laden with a sense of uncertainty that mirrored the shadows that danced across the walls.

Sarah, usually resolute, found herself grappling with similar doubts. "I can't shake the feeling that we're just scratching the surface, that there's a deeper level of deception we haven't uncovered."

The shadows of doubt cast a pall over their determination, their pursuit of truth clouded by the specter of uncertainty. Each revelation, once a beacon of clarity, now seemed like another layer in the Puppet Master's intricate tapestry of manipulation.

In a desperate attempt to dispel their doubts, they revisited the remnants of their investigation, scouring through notes and clues scattered across the room. However, every piece of evidence seemed to cast elongated shadows of suspicion, leaving them second-guessing their every conclusion.

The city outside whispered with echoes of uncertainty, its streets lined with shadows that seemed to hold secrets yet to be unveiled. Lucas and Sarah grappled with the unsettling realization that they might be mere pawns in the Puppet Master's relentless game of deception.

As evening descended, casting the apartment in a dim light, an unexpected visitor knocked on the door—a figure cloaked in shadows, their presence an enigmatic silhouette against the faint glow from the hallway.

Lucas hesitated, his hand hovering over the doorknob, the shadows of doubt casting a veil of caution over his instincts. Yet, curiosity outweighed apprehension as he opened the door, inviting the visitor into the uncertain confines of their investigation.

The figure stepped into the room, their features obscured by darkness, but an air of familiarity lingered in their presence. A voice, tinged with an otherworldly resonance, pierced the silence.

"I've seen the shadows that cloud your minds," the figure spoke, their words weaving a cryptic melody. "But not all is lost in the labyrinth of doubt."

Their enigmatic visitor revealed fragments of obscured truths, each sentence a glimmer of illumination amidst the darkness that had enveloped Lucas and Sarah. The visitor's revelations hinted at a path forward—a hidden thread that, if followed, could lead them out of the shadows of doubt and closer to the heart of the Puppet Master's elusive schemes.

As the visitor vanished into the night, leaving behind cryptic guidance, Lucas and Sarah found a flicker of hope amidst the shadows. Though doubts lingered, a newfound resolve simmered within them—a determination to pierce through the veil of uncertainty and confront the looming convergence that awaited, seeking to unearth the truth buried within the shadows of doubt.

Chapter 8

Chapter 8: "Unveiling the Enigma"

Following the cryptic guidance from their enigmatic visitor, Lucas Black and Sarah Martinez embarked on a new phase of their investigation—one aimed at unraveling the enigma of the Puppet Master's elusive schemes. The shadows of doubt still lingered, but a newfound determination burned within them, propelling their pursuit of truth forward.

In the heart of the city, amidst the bustling streets and looming skyscrapers, Lucas and Sarah retraced their steps, revisiting key locations that had been pivotal in their investigation. Each place held fragments of the Puppet Master's influence—cryptic symbols etched into walls, remnants of illusions, and traces of manipulation that lingered in the air.

The guidance provided by their mysterious visitor had led them to a secluded archive—an ancient repository of forgotten knowledge hidden beneath layers of obscurity. Dust-covered tomes and crumbling manuscripts awaited their exploration, their pages harboring secrets that held the promise of unveiling the enigma that had eluded them.

Pages turned, revealing arcane passages and esoteric texts that spoke of powers beyond comprehension. The Puppet Master's name appeared in cryptic contexts, woven into the narratives of ancient prophecies and clandestine rituals.

Amidst the labyrinthine corridors of knowledge, they stumbled upon a tome that seemed to pulsate with an other-worldly energy. Its cover adorned with symbols that resonated with familiarity—a resonance that echoed through their memories of the Puppet Master's machinations.

As they delved into the depths of the tome, deciphering its cryptic contents, a revelation emerged—a convergence, foretold in the annals of ancient prophecy, where the boundaries between worlds would blur, and the Puppet Master's ultimate agenda would come to fruition.

The enigma began to unravel before their eyes, the threads of deception and manipulation slowly revealing a tapestry woven with a purpose both intricate and foreboding. The convergence stood as the focal point—a nexus where the Puppet Master's designs would culminate, setting the stage for a cataclysmic event that would shape the very fabric of reality.

Armed with newfound knowledge, Lucas and Sarah pieced together the fragments of prophecy, mapping out a course that would lead them to the epicenter of the looming convergence. Their pursuit of truth had taken on a renewed fervor, guided by the cryptic revelations and the urgency to prevent the Puppet Master's plans from coming to fruition.

As the city slumbered in the embrace of night, Lucas and Sarah set out on their final journey, determined to confront the enigma that had plagued their investigation. The looming convergence beckoned—an enigmatic event that held the key to unraveling the Puppet Master's grand design, and they stood ready to face the ultimate challenge in their quest to unveil the enigma and thwart the Puppet Master's insidious plot.

Chapter 9

Chapter 9: "The Labyrinthine Trap"

Lucas Black and Sarah Martinez ventured into the heart of the city, their minds tethered to the prophecy that foretold the looming convergence—the climax of the Puppet Master's intricate machinations. Every step they took felt like a plunge into a labyrinthine trap, a maze designed to ensnare their resolve and test their determination.

Their journey led them through obscure alleyways and forgotten avenues, each path shrouded in an eerie silence that whispered of impending chaos. The city, a canvas for the Puppet Master's illusions, seemed to shift and distort around them, creating a disorienting labyrinth of streets and structures.

As they navigated through the labyrinth of uncertainty, cryptic symbols adorned the walls, a foreboding prelude to the convergence that loomed on the horizon. Each symbol seemed to beckon them forward, drawing them deeper into the intricate trap woven by their elusive adversary.

The city's geography twisted and contorted, morphing into an enigmatic puzzle that challenged their perceptions. Every turn led them further into the maze—a maze where reality intertwined with illusion, blurring the lines between truth and deception.

Amidst the disorienting labyrinth, they encountered obstacles crafted by the Puppet Master's design—hallucinatory apparitions, echoes of past illusions, and whispers that played tricks on their minds. The labyrinthine trap tested their resolve, coaxing them to lose themselves in the maze's intricate corridors.

Yet, driven by determination and guided by the fragments of prophecy they had unearthed, Lucas and Sarah pressed on, their senses heightened and their minds focused on the ultimate goal—to reach the epicenter of the convergence before the Puppet Master's grand design unfolded.

The cityscape shifted once more, revealing a hidden passage—an entrance to a realm that existed beyond the veil of reality. An ethereal glow emanated from the entrance, a beacon drawing them closer to the heart of the labyrinthine trap.

With hesitant steps, they crossed the threshold, entering a surreal landscape—a realm where the laws of reality were suspended, and the Puppet Master's influence reigned supreme. A myriad of illusions danced before their eyes, weaving a tapestry of dissonant images that sought to ensnare their minds.

Their determination wavered amidst the cacophony of illusions, but the echoes of the prophecy echoed in their minds, urging them to persevere. With steadfast resolve, Lucas and Sarah pressed forward, maneuvering through the labyrinthine trap with unwavering determination.

At the convergence's epicenter, a pulsating vortex materialized—a gateway to the culmination of the Puppet Master's intricate schemes. The air crackled with an otherworldly energy, and the labyrinthine trap seemed to converge upon this focal point, entangling their fate with the Puppet Master's ultimate design.

Standing on the precipice of the vortex, Lucas and Sarah prepared to confront the enigma that had eluded them—a showdown that would test their will, their bond, and their resolve to thwart the Puppet Master's insidious plans and emerge from the labyrinthine trap victorious.

Chapter 10

Chapter 10: "Whispers in the Dark"

In the throes of the Puppet Master's labyrinthine trap, Lucas Black and Sarah Martinez stood at the brink of the pulsating vortex—the epicenter of the impending convergence. The air hummed with an eerie resonance, and ethereal whispers echoed in the dark, teasing their senses with elusive secrets.

As they gazed into the swirling abyss, shadows danced at the periphery of their vision, casting doubt upon their resolve. Whispers echoed from the depths of the vortex, fragments of cryptic messages that tantalized and unsettled.

Lucas and Sarah exchanged a knowing glance, their determination fortified by the bonds of their shared pursuit. With each step toward the vortex, the whispers intensified, urging caution and sowing seeds of uncertainty.

The realm within the vortex was a tapestry of shifting illusions—an intricate web woven from the fabric of their fears and desires. The echoes of voices, both familiar and unknown, reverberated through the darkness, creating an enigmatic symphony that tested their resolve.

Amidst the dissonance of whispers, fragments of memories surfaced—a mosaic of their journey through the Puppet Master's labyrinth. Illusions manifested, teasing their perceptions with echoes of past encounters and enigmatic symbols that danced in the darkness.

The whispers seemed to carry fragments of truth, veiled in cryptic riddles and elusive promises. Echoes of warnings and prophecies intertwined, painting a mosaic of conflicting truths and deceptive lies.

With each whisper, doubt gnawed at their determination, threatening to unravel their resolve in the face of the unknown. Yet, their shared determination anchored them, a beacon amidst the shadowy chaos that enveloped them.

In a moment of clarity, Sarah's voice cut through the whispers, resolute and unwavering. "We cannot let these whispers cloud our purpose. We must push forward, together."

With renewed determination, they pressed on, navigating through the cacophony of whispers that sought to mislead and confuse. Lucas and Sarah clung to the fragments of truth within the whispers, piecing together a path toward the heart of the vortex.

At the vortex's core, a figure materialized—a spectral apparition cloaked in shadows. The whispers intensified, resonating with an ominous resonance as the figure beckoned them closer, its presence a manifestation of the Puppet Master's enigmatic influence.

With a final surge of determination, Lucas and Sarah confronted the spectral figure, their wills united against the whispers that sought to unravel their resolve. The figure shimmered, its illusion fading away to reveal a truth hidden in plain sight—an illusion crafted by the Puppet Master's mastery over the mind.

As the whispers subsided, clarity emerged. Lucas and Sarah stood united, their bond unbroken amidst the echoes of deception and truth. The enigmatic whispers in the dark had tested their resolve, but they emerged stronger, ready to face the impending convergence with unwavering determination.

Chapter 11

Chapter 11: "Playing the Player."

The lingering aftermath of the vortex encounter had left Lucas Black and Sarah Martinez grappling with a newfound clarity amidst the lingering echoes of the Puppet Master's illusions. As they regrouped in the dimly lit precinct office, a sense of determination permeated the air—a resolve to turn the tables and play the Puppet Master's game on their terms.

Lucas sat at his desk, a map spread out before him, a web of connections and symbols charting the Puppet Master's maneuvers. Sarah, her gaze fixed on the array of cryptic messages they had amassed, meticulously dissected the enigmatic clues that littered their investigation.

"We've been reactive for too long," Lucas muttered, his voice tinged with determination. "It's time we take control, play the player."

Sarah nodded in agreement, her eyes gleaming with a newfound sense of purpose. "We need to anticipate the next move, understand the patterns, and outmaneuver the Puppet Master at their own game."

Their investigation had transitioned from a pursuit of truth to a strategic game of cat and mouse—a high-stakes endeavor where deciphering the Puppet Master's motives became paramount. They scrutinized every detail, from the faintest whispers to the intricate symbols that had permeated their journey, seeking the thread that would unravel the Puppet Master's elusive game.

Their plan began to take shape—a calculated gambit that aimed to lure the Puppet Master into revealing their hand. Lucas and Sarah strategized, analyzing the patterns and psychological cues embedded within the Puppet Master's manipulations, crafting an intricate plan to exploit their adversary's own methods against them.

As night descended upon the city once more, Lucas and Sarah set their plan into motion. They left behind breadcrumbs of cryptic messages and veiled hints, designed to pique the Puppet Master's curiosity and draw them into the intricate dance of deception they had orchestrated.

The city streets became their stage—a battleground where truth and illusion intersected, blurring the lines between hunter and hunted. They meticulously maneuvered through the shadows, their every move a calculated step towards turning the tables on the Puppet Master.

Whispers of their plan echoed through the city, reaching the ears of their elusive adversary. The Puppet Master, ensconced in their web of illusions, appeared intrigued by the challenge Lucas and Sarah presented—a challenge that demanded the Puppet Master's adeptness to be tested against their own game.

With each passing moment, the tension mounted. Lucas and Sarah waited, their breaths held in anticipation, as the Puppet Master's response unfolded—a carefully orchestrated maneuver designed to outwit their adversary's moves and reclaim control of the ever-shifting power dynamics.

The Puppet Master's counterplay revealed itself—an intricate web of illusions that teased at the edges of their plan. The cityscape became an elaborate chessboard where each move held consequences, and Lucas and Sarah found themselves ensnared in a game of psychological warfare with their adversary.

As the night wore on, the game escalated—a battle of wits that intensified with each strategic move. The city buzzed with whispers of the escalating conflict, the stakes raised to a crescendo that demanded a decisive outcome.

Lucas and Sarah remained steadfast, their determination unyielding as they anticipated the Puppet Master's next calculated move. They played the player, maneuvering through the intricacies of the game, poised for the critical moment that would tip the scales in their favor and ultimately unravel the Puppet Master's elusive stratagem.

Chapter 12

Chapter 12: "In the Clutches of Obsession"

The relentless cat-and-mouse game with the Puppet Master had plunged Lucas Black and Sarah Martinez into a relentless pursuit—a pursuit that bordered on obsession. The intricate dance of strategy and deception had become an all-consuming endeavor, each move a calculated step deeper into the Puppet Master's labyrinth of manipulation.

Days blurred into nights as they chased elusive trails, deciphering cryptic messages and navigating through a city shrouded in uncertainty. Lucas and Sarah were ensnared in a web of their own making, their focus fixated on anticipating the Puppet Master's next move, often at the expense of their own well-being.

Sleep became a fleeting luxury, their minds consumed by the relentless pursuit of unraveling the Puppet Master's schemes. The city's rhythms echoed with their obsession, their thoughts consumed by the elusive figure orchestrating the intricate game they were entangled in.

Their investigation room transformed into a collage of clues and fragmented messages, an intricate mosaic that mirrored the depths of their obsession. The walls were adorned with cryptic symbols and interconnected threads—a visual representation of their relentless pursuit to outmaneuver the Puppet Master.

Lucas's gaze bore the weight of sleepless nights, his mind entrenched in decoding the Puppet Master's labyrinthine designs. Sarah, her determination unyielding, delved deeper into the psychological intricacies woven into their adversary's manipulations.

Whispers of concern echoed among their colleagues, veiled worries for their well-being amidst the all-consuming obsession that gripped Lucas and Sarah. The line between determination and fixation blurred, leaving them teetering on the edge of a consuming preoccupation with their elusive adversary.

Their pursuit of the Puppet Master had become a personal crusade, an obsession that eclipsed all else. Lucas and Sarah were entrenched in a relentless cycle of deciphering cryptic messages, analyzing patterns, and strategizing their next moves, driven by an insatiable need to outwit their elusive adversary.

Their lives had become intertwined with the Puppet Master's machinations, every waking moment consumed by thoughts of unraveling the enigmatic figure's designs. The boundary between reality and obsession blurred, leaving them ensnared in a labyrinth of their own making—a maze of relentless pursuit that threatened to consume them whole.

As they delved deeper into the Puppet Master's web, a realization dawned—an acknowledgment that their relentless pursuit had led them into the clutches of an all-consuming obsession. The Puppet Master's manipulations had taken on a life of their own, weaving into the very fabric of their existence, ensnaring their thoughts and actions.

Lucas and Sarah found themselves at a crossroads, confronted by the harsh truth of their obsessive pursuit. The relentless chase for the elusive adversary had taken a toll—a toll on their mental fortitude, their relationships, and their very identity. In the clutches of obsession, they stood on the precipice, grappling with the daunting realization that their relentless pursuit had veered dangerously close to losing themselves in the Puppet Master's intricate game.

Chapter 13

Chapter 13: "The Mental Gambit"

Lucas Black and Sarah Martinez found themselves at a critical juncture, grappling with the consuming obsession that had entangled them in the Puppet Master's intricate game. Recognizing the peril of their fixation, they sought to recalibrate their approach, to turn the tide of the mental gambit they were ensnared in.

In the somber silence of Lucas's apartment, they confronted the daunting truth that their relentless pursuit had become a dangerous mental gambit. The room, once adorned with cryptic clues, now stood devoid of the elaborate strings and symbols—a stark reflection of their determination to break free from the Puppet Master's web of manipulation.

"We've lost sight of ourselves in this chase," Sarah confessed, her voice tinged with a hint of remorse. "Our obsession has blurred the line between truth and illusion, leading us deeper into the Puppet Master's game."

Lucas nodded in agreement, the weight of their fixation evident in the lines etched upon his face. "We need to shift our focus, regain control of the mental gambit. Let's reassess our strategy and approach this from a different angle."

They retreated from the relentless pursuit, opting for introspection and deliberation. Lucas and Sarah sought solace in moments of respite, away from the relentless whispers and enigmatic clues that had consumed their thoughts.

In their pursuit of clarity, they revisited their initial clues, reevaluating the patterns and nuances they had uncovered throughout their investigation. The mental gambit they faced demanded a strategic retreat, a recalibration of their approach to outmaneuver the Puppet Master's machinations.

As they delved into the recesses of their memories, fragments of forgotten truths emerged—a mosaic of moments that had been overshadowed by their all-consuming obsession. The mental gambit they faced demanded a shift in perspective—a recognition that victory lay not in chasing illusions but in reclaiming their own clarity of purpose.

Their renewed approach revolved around regaining control, focusing on understanding rather than obsessing over the Puppet Master's every move. Lucas and Sarah sought a balance—a delicate equilibrium that would allow them to anticipate the adversary's maneuvers without succumbing to the siren call of obsession.

Days turned into weeks as they meticulously reevaluated their investigation, extracting essential truths from the myriad illusions woven by the Puppet Master. The mental gambit demanded resilience and restraint, an acknowledgment that clarity was their most potent weapon against the enigmatic adversary.

With each passing moment of introspection, Lucas and Sarah unearthed fragments of their own strength—the resilience that had fueled their pursuit of truth before it became consumed by obsession. The mental gambit slowly shifted in their favor, as they rekindled their determination to confront the Puppet Master with clarity and precision.

Armed with newfound resolve and a recalibrated strategy, Lucas and Sarah prepared to reenter the game—a game where the mental gambit demanded strategic maneuvering and a steadfast resolve to navigate the intricate labyrinth of deception while safeguarding their own sanity against the Puppet Master's relentless manipulations.

Chapter 14

Chapter 14: "Into the Abyss of Fear"

Lucas Black and Sarah Martinez stood on the precipice of a daunting reality—a reality that led them into the abyss of fear, a domain where the Puppet Master's manipulations delved into the depths of their most profound anxieties.

The mental gambit they had employed to recalibrate their approach had plunged them into uncharted territory, a realm where the Puppet Master's illusions preyed upon their deepest fears. Every step forward seemed to echo with a foreboding sense of trepidation, a reminder of the risks they faced in their pursuit of the elusive adversary.

Their investigation led them into a disconcerting realm—a desolate expanse where reality fractured and illusions thrived. Shadows danced on the edges of their perception, whispers of insecurities reverberated through the darkness, each echo a manifestation of the Puppet Master's mastery over their fears.

Lucas and Sarah found themselves confronted by apparitions that mirrored their deepest anxieties—manifestations crafted by the Puppet Master's malevolent design. The abyss of fear seemed to echo with taunting whispers, amplifying their vulnerabilities and exploiting the fractures in their resolve.

As they navigated through the abyss, echoes of past traumas surfaced—phantoms from their personal histories that had been skillfully woven into the Puppet Master's illusions. The weight of unresolved fears threatened to overshadow their determination, testing their resilience in the face of relentless psychological warfare.

Lucas clenched his jaw, his resolve faltering momentarily as visions of his past failures materialized before him. Sarah, too, found herself grappling with haunting specters from her own history, the illusions playing on her deepest insecurities.

Amidst the shadows that danced in the abyss of fear, a flicker of realization emerged. Lucas and Sarah recognized the Puppet Master's tactic—an attempt to exploit their vulnerabilities, to erode their determination by preying upon their fears.

With a shared resolve born from understanding, Lucas and Sarah confronted the illusions that loomed before them. They anchored themselves in their mutual determination, drawing strength from their bond and a shared purpose— to confront the abyss of fear and emerge stronger from its depths.

Their steps became deliberate, their movements calculated to unravel the illusions that haunted the abyss. With every confrontation, they peeled back the layers of fear, dispelling the Puppet Master's manipulations and reclaiming control over their own anxieties.

Through sheer resilience and an unwavering unity, Lucas and Sarah pressed on, challenging the illusions that sought to cripple their resolve. The echoes of their fears gradually diminished, replaced by a resolute determination to confront the Puppet Master on their terms.

As they navigated through the treacherous depths of the abyss, Lucas and Sarah emerged emboldened, their unity an impenetrable shield against the Puppet Master's attempts to exploit their vulnerabilities. The confrontation with their fears had strengthened their resolve, preparing them for the inevitable showdown that awaited—a confrontation that would test their mettle and determination as they ventured deeper into the labyrinth of the Puppet Master's manipulative designs.

Chapter 15

Chapter 15: "Confronting the Phantom"

The relentless pursuit through the abyss of fear had fortified Lucas Black and Sarah Martinez, their resilience tested and their determination unwavering. As they emerged from the haunting depths, they stood on the cusp of confronting the Phantom—the elusive Puppet Master whose machinations had woven an intricate tapestry of manipulation and illusion.

In the heart of the city, an abandoned theater stood as the chosen battleground—a symbolic arena where reality and illusion merged, where the final confrontation with the Phantom would unfold. The dilapidated walls echoed with whispers of anticipation, each creak and shuffle a prelude to the impending showdown.

Lucas and Sarah approached the theater, their resolve a palpable force amidst the eerie silence that enveloped the forsaken structure. The air crackled with anticipation, the lingering echoes of their harrowing journey through the abyss of fear serving as a testament to their unwavering determination.

As they stepped into the theater's hollowed halls, a haunting atmosphere surrounded them—a symphony of whispers and phantom echoes that reverberated through the desolate corridors. Illusions flickered in the corners of their vision, remnants of the Puppet Master's malevolent designs.

At the center of the theater's grand stage, a spectral figure materialized—the Phantom, cloaked in enigmatic shadows that seemed to defy the laws of reality. The air grew heavy with an ominous presence, the silence pregnant with the anticipation of the inevitable clash between adversaries.

"We've danced to your tune long enough," Lucas's voice echoed with a steely resolve, cutting through the phantom whispers that echoed within the theater. "It's time to reveal yourself and put an end to this charade."

Sarah's gaze bore into the darkness, her voice carrying an unwavering determination. "Your illusions won't hold us captive any longer. We've come to confront the Phantom—the mastermind behind this relentless game."

The Phantom's presence seemed to ripple with a malevolent energy, a silent acknowledgment of the impending confrontation. Illusions wove around the spectral figure, flickering like phantoms in the dim light—a testament to the Puppet Master's mastery in manipulating perception.

Lucas and Sarah stood united, their bond an unyielding force against the Phantom's machinations. With every step forward, their determination grew, each movement a testament to their resilience in the face of the Puppet Master's illusions.

As the standoff reached its crescendo, Lucas and Sarah launched their final gambit—a gambit forged from unity and clarity of purpose. They confronted the Phantom with unwavering resolve, exposing the illusions and piercing through the shadows that had veiled their adversary's true identity.

In a dramatic revelation, the Phantom's illusions shattered, unveiling a figure—a mere mortal ensnared by their own obsessions and manipulative designs. The grandeur of the Puppet Master diminished, revealing the vulnerability that lay beneath the enigmatic façade.

The theater echoed with the dissolution of illusions, the shattered fragments falling to the ground like remnants of a vanishing specter. Lucas and Sarah stood amidst the dissipating echoes, their confrontation with the Phantom marking the climax of their relentless battle against manipulation and deceit.

With the revelation of the Phantom's true identity, Lucas and Sarah emerged victorious—not merely in defeating an adversary but in reclaiming their clarity of purpose and unity amidst the labyrinth of the Puppet Master's intricate game. The showdown had ended, leaving behind a resounding truth—their unyielding determination had prevailed, unraveling the illusions and confronting the phantom that had haunted their relentless pursuit of truth.

Chapter 16

Chapter 16: "The Charade Unmasked"

In the aftermath of the confrontation with the Phantom, Lucas Black and Sarah Martinez stood amidst the dissipating remnants of illusions, their minds reeling from the revelation that had unveiled the true identity of their elusive adversary.

The theater, once a stage for enigmatic illusions, now bore witness to the revelation—a shattered charade that lay scattered like debris across the floor. The Phantom's manipulative masquerade had come to an end, exposing the frailty of the figure behind the elaborate illusions.

As the echoes of the confrontation lingered in the hollowed halls, Lucas and Sarah faced the revelation with a mix of astonishment and understanding. The adversary they had pursued with unwavering determination stood unmasked—

an individual consumed by obsessions and driven to manipulate the fabric of reality.

"We were ensnared by the manipulations of an individual plagued by their own insecurities," Lucas mused, the weight of the revelation evident in his voice. "The Puppet Master's illusions were a facade to conceal their own vulnerabilities."

Sarah nodded in agreement, her gaze fixated on the remnants of the shattered illusions. "Their obsession with control led them to weave intricate deceptions, blurring the lines between reality and illusion."

The charade had been unmasked, leaving behind a sense of empathy for the once-elusive adversary. The Phantom's manipulative designs, born from their own fears and insecurities, had ensnared Lucas and Sarah in a relentless game of psychological warfare.

As they surveyed the theater, the truth resonated—the pursuit of truth had led them through a labyrinth of deception, but in unmasking the Phantom, they had discovered a shared understanding of the vulnerabilities that had driven their adversary's manipulations.

Their journey, though riddled with illusions and manipulation, had forged an unbreakable bond—an alliance that transcended the complexities of the Phantom's game. Lucas and Sarah emerged from the confrontation with newfound clarity, their shared experiences solidifying their resolve to confront the truth, no matter the adversities they faced.

With a sense of closure, they left the theater, the echoes of the confrontation fading into the city's bustling rhythm. The charade had ended, leaving behind the remnants of an adversary whose illusions had once veiled their true identity.

Lucas and Sarah stepped into the night, their minds freed from the Puppet Master's manipulative grasp. As they walked away from the theater, the shadows of the Phantom's illusions dissipated, leaving behind a path illuminated by the clarity of truth and a renewed determination to navigate the complexities of life without succumbing to the allure of manipulative illusions.

Chapter 17: "The Haunting Echoes"

In the wake of their confrontation with the unmasked Phantom, Lucas Black and Sarah Martinez found themselves grappling with haunting echoes of their journey. The remnants of the Puppet Master's illusions lingered, casting spectral shadows across their thoughts and memories.

Days turned into nights, yet the echoes of their relentless pursuit reverberated within their minds. The memories of illusions and manipulations continued to haunt them, lingering like ghostly apparitions in the corners of their consciousness.

Lucas paced the confines of his apartment, his thoughts consumed by the haunting echoes of their encounter. The remnants of the Phantom's illusions danced in his mind, teasing at the edges of his perception and leaving behind an indelible imprint.

Sarah, too, found herself ensnared by the haunting echoes of their pursuit. Her nights were restless, plagued by visions of the labyrinthine traps they had navigated, each illusion a haunting reminder of the psychological warfare they had endured.

Their shared experiences had forged an unbreakable bond, but the lingering specters of the Puppet Master's manipulations tested the resilience of their resolve. The haunting echoes threatened to overshadow their victory, casting doubts on the clarity they had fought so hard to attain.

As they sought solace in the tranquility of the city's night, the echoes persisted—a relentless reminder of their arduous journey. The bustling streets whispered tales of their confrontation, the remnants of the Puppet Master's illusions a spectral presence that seemed to linger in every shadow and flickering light.

In a moment of shared reflection, Lucas and Sarah confronted the haunting echoes that pervaded their thoughts. They sought to acknowledge the weight of their experiences, recognizing that the remnants of the Phantom's illusions were not easily dispelled.

Their confrontation with the Puppet Master had left an indelible mark, a haunting reminder of the complexities of truth and deception. Yet, within the haunting echoes lay a testament to their resilience—their unwavering determination to confront the illusions and emerge stronger from the labyrinth of manipulation.

With a shared understanding, Lucas and Sarah embraced the haunting echoes as reminders of their shared journey—a journey that had tested their mettle, forged their bond, and ultimately led them to the truth. They found solace in each other's company, drawing strength from their shared experiences and the resolve that had guided them through the relentless pursuit of truth amidst the haunting echoes of the Puppet Master's manipulations.

Chapter 18

Chapter 18: "Trapped in Illusion"

Lucas Black and Sarah Martinez found themselves in the aftermath of their haunting confrontation with the Phantom, still grappling with the lingering remnants of illusions that seemed to ensnare their thoughts and perceptions.

Their pursuit of truth had led them through a labyrinth of manipulations, and despite unmasking the Phantom's true identity, the echoes of the Puppet Master's illusions persisted. Days turned into a relentless cycle of uncertainty, each moment shadowed by the remnants of the enigmatic adversary's deceptions.

Lucas retreated into solitude, seeking respite from the relentless echoes of illusion that pervaded his thoughts. The familiar confines of his sanctuary offered no solace as the lingering visions of the Puppet Master's manipulations continued to haunt his mind.

Sarah, too, found herself trapped in the labyrinth of illusion. The city's streets, once familiar and comforting, now seemed distorted, carrying echoes of past illusions that teased at the edges of her perception.

The lines between reality and illusion blurred, casting doubts on their perceptions and leaving them ensnared in a web woven by the Phantom's manipulative designs. The relentless pursuit had taken its toll, leaving them questioning the very fabric of their reality.

As they navigated through the city's enigmatic maze, whispers of doubt intensified. The remnants of illusions manifested around them, fragments of past encounters with the Phantom echoing through the bustling streets, further entangling their minds in the intricate web of deception.

In a moment of shared vulnerability, Lucas and Sarah acknowledged the depths of their entrapment in illusion. They recognized that the pursuit of truth had led them into a labyrinth where the lines between reality and deception had become perilously thin.

Together, they sought clarity amidst the mire of illusion, piecing together fragments of truth from the echoes that reverberated through their memories. Their bond, forged through adversity, became their anchor—a beacon of solidarity in the midst of the swirling illusions that threatened to consume their sanity.

With a shared determination, Lucas and Sarah resolved to confront the remnants of illusion that plagued their thoughts. They sought to dismantle the lingering echoes of the Puppet Master's manipulations, to navigate through the labyrinth and emerge with a clarity that would dispel the illusions that ensnared their minds.

Their journey through the labyrinth of illusion was fraught with uncertainty, but their shared resolve remained unyielding. Lucas and Sarah traversed the enigmatic landscape, determined to unravel the remnants of deception and reclaim their grasp on reality, forging a path toward clarity in the midst of the persistent echoes that continued to haunt their pursuit of truth.

Chapter 19

Chapter 19: "The Mind's Chessboard"

Lucas Black and Sarah Martinez found themselves in a perplexing state as they grappled with the remnants of illusion that pervaded their thoughts. Determined to break free from the haunting echoes of the Phantom's manipulations, they embarked on a journey through what felt like the mind's chessboard—a strategic landscape where clarity of thought and foresight became their allies.

Their pursuit of truth had transformed into a mental game, each move calculated as they navigated the complexities of perception and reality. The city, once a familiar landscape, now became an intricate chessboard where the Puppet Master's illusions served as strategic obstacles to overcome.

Lucas and Sarah approached their investigation as seasoned players, each step forward a deliberate move in their mental chess match against the remnants of illusion. They analyzed the remnants of the Phantom's manipulations, seeking patterns and deciphering the subtle cues embedded within the echoes that persisted.

In the quietude of their shared workspace, they strategized, meticulously mapping out their moves like players plotting their next maneuvers on a chessboard. The pursuit of truth had evolved into a cerebral battle—a match of wits against the enigmatic adversary who had ensnared them in a labyrinth of perception.

Their bond became their greatest strength, a unified front against the Puppet Master's remnants that lingered like pieces on the mind's chessboard. With each calculated move, they sought to dismantle the illusions and anticipate the Phantom's maneuvers, determined to emerge victorious from the mental labyrinth.

The city's streets served as the battleground for their mental chess match, each corner a potential trap, and each intersection a strategic point of consideration. Lucas and Sarah navigated through the urban landscape, their thoughts honed to decipher the complexities of the enigmatic game that surrounded them.

As they delved deeper into the mind's chessboard, a sense of clarity began to emerge—a gradual unraveling of the Phantom's remnants that had clouded their perceptions. The strategic maneuvers they employed started to reveal glimpses of truth amidst the remnants of illusion that lingered in the recesses of their minds.

Their unity and shared determination acted as a shield against the Puppet Master's lingering manipulations. With each strategic move, they advanced, piecing together the fragmented puzzle of illusion and deception, maneuvering through the mind's chessboard with a determination to reclaim their grasp on reality.

Lucas and Sarah's mental chess match with the remnants of the Phantom's illusions became a testament to their resilience—a testament to their unwavering pursuit of truth amidst the complexities of the mind's intricate game. As they navigated through the mental labyrinth, each move brought them closer to dispelling the illusions that had ensnared their thoughts and perceptions.

Chapter 20: "Schemes and Illusions"

Lucas Black and Sarah Martinez found themselves immersed in the intricacies of the Puppet Master's final schemes and illusions. Their mental chess match against the remnants of the Phantom's manipulations had brought them to the precipice of understanding, yet the elusive adversary continued to weave intricate illusions.

The city's landscape became a canvas for the Puppet Master's final act—a culmination of schemes and illusions that tested Lucas and Sarah's resolve. Shadows danced across the urban expanse, whispers of past encounters mingling with the present, each element meticulously orchestrated by the Phantom.

In the depths of their pursuit, Lucas and Sarah confronted enigmatic symbols and cryptic messages that peppered the cityscape. The remnants of the Phantom's manipulations seemed to intertwine with reality, blurring the lines between truth and illusion in a final attempt to obscure their adversaries' path.

The echoes of their mental chess match persisted, urging Lucas and Sarah to unravel the complexities of the Phantom's designs. They navigated through the intricate maze of illusions, dissecting each element with a meticulous eye, seeking patterns and vulnerabilities amidst the veils of deception.

Every encounter became a calculated maneuver, a strategic effort to dismantle the remnants of illusion that obscured their pursuit of truth. Lucas and Sarah moved with precision, anticipating the Puppet Master's schemes while safeguarding their perceptions against the lingering echoes of manipulation.

The Puppet Master's final illusions posed a formidable challenge, each mirage crafted with a cunning precision that tested the very limits of their determination. Yet, Lucas and Sarah remained resolute, their bond and shared determination serving as a beacon amidst the labyrinth of schemes and illusions.

With each passing moment, they pieced together fragments of truth from the intricate illusions that surrounded them. The city, once a playground for the Puppet Master's manipulations, became a battleground where their unity and clarity of purpose fortified their resolve against the enigmatic adversary's final gambit.

As they delved deeper into the Phantom's illusions, a sense of revelation began to emerge—a clarity that cut through the veil of deception, unraveling the complexities of the schemes woven by their elusive adversary. Lucas and Sarah maneuvered through the final layers of illusions, determined to confront the Puppet Master with a newfound understanding forged from the remnants of their relentless pursuit.

Chapter 21

Chapter 21: "The Tangled Threads."

Lucas Black and Sarah Martinez found themselves entrenched in the aftermath of the Puppet Master's final illusions. The city's labyrinthine streets echoed with the remnants of their elusive adversary's machinations, leaving behind a tapestry of tangled threads that obscured the path to resolution.

In the heart of their investigation room, the walls were adorned with a complex web of interconnected threads—a visual representation of the enigmatic schemes that had entangled their pursuit. Cryptic symbols and fragments of clues were woven together, a testament to the intricate nature of the Puppet Master's manipulations.

Lucas and Sarah meticulously dissected the tangled threads that littered their investigation board, each thread a representation of a clue or illusion woven into the complex tapestry. They sought to untangle the chaos, to discern patterns amidst the intricate web that obscured the truth they sought.

The tangled threads mirrored the complexities of their journey—a convergence of elusive clues and deceptive illusions that had led them through a labyrinth of uncertainty. Lucas and Sarah navigated through the maze of interconnected threads, seeking the pivotal connections that would unravel the enigmatic puzzle.

As they delved deeper into the tangled threads, a realization dawned—the Puppet Master's manipulations were interwoven with precision, each thread leading to another layer of complexity. Their pursuit of truth demanded a meticulous unraveling of the tangled web, a patient unraveling of the Puppet Master's intricate schemes.

Amidst the chaos of the investigation room, Lucas and Sarah's collaboration became the linchpin of their unraveling. They pieced together fragments of clues, drawing upon their shared experiences and insights to navigate through the tangled threads that obscured the path to resolution.

With every thread untangled, a fragment of truth emerged—a faint glimmer amidst the labyrinthine chaos. Lucas and Sarah persisted, their determination unyielding, as they painstakingly unraveled the tangled threads that concealed the elusive truth they sought.

Their pursuit through the tangled threads was a testament to their resilience, a relentless endeavor to confront the complexities of the Puppet Master's manipulations. As they continued their meticulous unraveling, a sense of clarity began to emerge, offering glimpses of the truth obscured within the convoluted tapestry woven by their elusive adversary.

Chapter 22

Chapter 22: "Pawns of Perception"

In the wake of unraveling the tangled threads left by the Puppet Master's manipulations, Lucas Black and Sarah Martinez found themselves confronted with a chilling revelation—they had been unwitting pawns in a game of perception carefully orchestrated by their elusive adversary.

The echoes of their pursuit reverberated through the city, whispers of their encounters with the Phantom and the remnants of illusions amplifying their realization. Lucas and Sarah grappled with the unsettling truth that their perceptions had been expertly manipulated, rendering them mere pawns in the Puppet Master's enigmatic game.

Their investigation room, once a sanctuary for deciphering clues, became a stark reminder of their role as pawns of perception. The walls bore witness to the tangled web of illusions they had unraveled, a silent testament to the intricacies of the Puppet Master's manipulative designs.

Lucas paced the confines of the room, his thoughts consumed by the unsettling revelation. "We've been maneuvered like pawns on a chessboard," he muttered, the weight of their unwitting role as instruments of the Phantom's manipulations evident in his voice.

Sarah nodded in solemn acknowledgment. "Our perceptions were expertly molded, guiding us through a maze of illusions and manipulating our actions at every turn."

The realization that they had been unwittingly steered through a maze of deceptive perceptions left Lucas and Sarah grappling with a profound sense of disquiet. Their pursuit of truth had been orchestrated by the Puppet Master's masterful manipulation of their perceptions, casting doubt on every decision they had made.

The city's streets, once a familiar landscape, now bore witness to the echoes of their role as pawns in the enigmatic game. Lucas and Sarah navigated through the urban expanse with newfound awareness, scrutinizing every detail with a discerning eye, wary of falling prey to further manipulations.

Their bond became a shield against the insidious nature of the Puppet Master's designs, a shared understanding that their perceptions had been toyed with, and their actions guided along a path forged by deceptive illusions. With each step forward, they sought to reclaim their agency, to shatter the confines of the roles imposed upon them.

Lucas and Sarah were determined to break free from the shackles of being pawns of perception. They vowed to navigate through the city's intricacies with a renewed sense of vigilance, relying on their unity and shared resolve to confront the Puppet Master's manipulations head-on, forging

their own path through the labyrinth of illusions that had
once ensnared them.

Chapter 23

Chapter 23: "The Illusionist's Dilemma"

Lucas Black and Sarah Martinez found themselves grappling with the enigmatic nature of the Illusionist's Dilemma —the moral quandary of discerning truth from deception in the wake of the Puppet Master's manipulations.

The remnants of illusions lingered like a haunting specter, casting doubt on the authenticity of their perceptions. The Illusionist's Dilemma weighed heavily on their minds as they navigated the city's labyrinth, haunted by the Puppet Master's legacy of deception.

Their pursuit of truth had led them through a maze of illusions, leaving behind a lingering sense of uncertainty. Lucas and Sarah confronted the paradox of discerning reality from the remnants of the Phantom's manipulative designs, each encounter fraught with the Illusionist's Dilemma.

As they retraced their steps through the city, Lucas and Sarah sought to dissect the layers of illusion that shrouded their perceptions. They grappled with the moral ambiguity of their journey, questioning the authenticity of every clue and fragment they encountered.

The Illusionist's Dilemma tested their resolve, challenging them to differentiate between truth and deceptive mirages. Every encounter became a puzzle—a delicate balance between skepticism and trust, as they sought to unravel the remnants of the Puppet Master's manipulations without succumbing to uncertainty.

Their pursuit was fraught with moral complexities—a struggle to decipher the genuine from the illusory, to discern the authenticity of their perceptions amidst the lingering echoes of deception. Lucas and Sarah sought to navigate through the Illusionist's Dilemma with a clarity that eluded them, wary of falling prey to the manipulative designs that had once ensnared their thoughts.

In their quest for truth, they grappled with the shadows of doubt, acknowledging that the Illusionist's Dilemma was an integral part of their journey—a test of their resilience and discernment amidst the echoes of the Phantom's illusions.

Lucas and Sarah's determination to confront the Illusionist's Dilemma was unwavering. With each step forward, they honed their instincts, relying on their shared experiences and the strength of their bond to guide them through the enigmatic landscape of perceptions and illusions.

Their pursuit through the Illusionist's Dilemma was a testament to their unwavering resolve—a relentless quest to pierce through the deceptive veils and reclaim their grasp on reality. As they grappled with the complexities of discerning truth from deception, Lucas and Sarah remained steadfast, determined to confront the Illusionist's Dilemma head-on and emerge stronger from the echoes of the Puppet Master's manipulations.

Chapter 24

Chapter 24: "Abyss of the Unknown"

Lucas Black and Sarah Martinez found themselves teetering on the brink of the Abyss of the Unknown—a precipice where the boundaries between truth and obscurity blurred, casting their pursuit into an enigmatic chasm of uncertainty.

The remnants of the Puppet Master's manipulations echoed through the city, leaving behind a haunting sense of ambiguity. Lucas and Sarah confronted the Abyss of the Unknown, grappling with the unsettling realization that the answers they sought might lie in the uncharted territories of the unknown.

Their investigation room became a sanctuary for contemplation, adorned with fragments of clues and cryptic symbols that spoke of an elusive truth concealed within the depths of uncertainty. The city, once a familiar backdrop, now bore witness to their quest, a terrain fraught with shadows of the unknown.

Lucas paced the confines of the room, his mind wrestling with the complexities of the Abyss of the Unknown. "Every step forward feels like we're descending deeper into obscurity," he mused, the weight of uncertainty evident in his voice.

Sarah nodded in solemn agreement. "The more we seek answers, the more the unknown seems to expand, shrouding the truth in a veil of ambiguity."

Their pursuit through the Abyss of the Unknown was a daunting endeavor, a relentless journey into uncharted territories where clarity seemed elusive. Lucas and Sarah navigated through the urban expanse, their thoughts ensnared by the echoes of ambiguity that loomed like a specter, obscuring the path to resolution.

Every clue they uncovered seemed to unveil more questions than answers, leading them further into the depths of uncertainty. The city's labyrinth became a metaphor for their quest—a maze of twists and turns that obscured the elusive truth they sought.

In their pursuit through the Abyss of the Unknown, Lucas and Sarah leaned on each other, finding solace in their shared determination amidst the ambiguity. Their bond became a guiding light, a beacon of unity in the face of the uncertainties that clouded their path.

With each moment in the unknown, they honed their instincts, navigating through the shadows with a cautious resolve. The answers they sought seemed to linger just beyond their grasp, tantalizingly close yet veiled in the enigmatic depths of uncertainty.

As they delved deeper into the Abyss of the Unknown, Lucas and Sarah confronted their fears of obscurity, embracing the uncertainty as an integral part of their journey. Their relentless pursuit persisted, fueled by an unwavering determination to unravel the mysteries that lay hidden within the uncharted territories, forging ahead into the unknown with a shared commitment to confront the obscurities and emerge stronger from the enigmatic depths they ventured into.

Chapter 25

Chapter 25: "Dance of Deception"

Lucas Black and Sarah Martinez found themselves entangled in the Dance of Deception—a relentless and intricate performance orchestrated by the echoes of the Puppet Master's manipulations.

The city's streets, once familiar, now seemed to twist and contort, echoing with the remnants of the Phantom's illusions. Lucas and Sarah navigated through the urban expanse, keenly aware of the deceptive choreography that surrounded them.

Each step they took became a calculated move in this elusive dance, a delicate balance between uncovering truth and avoiding the seductive allure of deceptive mirages. The Dance of Deception tested their instincts, inviting them to discern the genuine from the illusory.

Their investigation room, a sanctuary for deciphering clues, bore witness to the intricate steps of the Dance of Deception. Fragments of evidence were strewn across the walls—a mosaic of cryptic symbols and elusive clues that seemed to sway to the rhythm of the Phantom's enigmatic performance.

Lucas and Sarah grappled with the complexities of the Dance of Deception, recognizing that every move they made could be a step closer to clarity or a spiral into further ambiguity. The echoes of the Puppet Master's manipulations whispered through the labyrinthine corridors of their thoughts, urging caution and skepticism at every turn.

As they ventured deeper into the Dance of Deception, Lucas and Sarah sharpened their senses, honing their instincts to discern the intricacies of the enigmatic choreography. They sought patterns within the dance, striving to uncover the underlying truth amidst the Phantom's intricate performance.

Their unity became their greatest asset in navigating the Dance of Deception. Lucas and Sarah synchronized their steps, relying on their shared experiences and mutual trust to guide them through the deceptive labyrinth that surrounded their pursuit.

In the heart of the city's complexities, Lucas and Sarah embraced the nuances of the Dance of Deception—a testament to their resilience and determination to confront the manipulative illusions that entrapped them. Their pursuit through the deceptive choreography was an unwavering endeavor, a relentless dance where each move brought them closer to unraveling the elusive truth hidden within the echoes of the Phantom's intricate performance.

Chapter 26

Chapter 26: "Unraveling the Mirage"

Lucas Black and Sarah Martinez, resolute in their quest for truth amidst the Dance of Deception, found themselves on the cusp of unraveling the Mirage—a pivotal moment in their relentless pursuit.

The city's landscape seemed to shimmer with deceptive allure, the echoes of the Puppet Master's illusions casting a veil of ambiguity. Lucas and Sarah navigated through the urban expanse, their senses heightened, attuned to the subtle nuances that hinted at the Mirage's unraveling.

Their investigation room, a haven amidst the city's complexities, bore witness to the meticulous unraveling of the Mirage. Fragments of clues and cryptic symbols adorned the walls, a mosaic of enigmatic patterns that beckoned to be deciphered, promising glimpses of the elusive truth.

Lucas and Sarah scrutinized every detail, piecing together fragments of evidence in a concerted effort to decode the Mirage. Their determination served as a beacon, guiding them through the intricate dance of illusions and manipulation orchestrated by the elusive Phantom.

As they delved deeper into the Mirage, a sense of clarity began to emerge—a revelation born from their meticulous unraveling of the enigmatic patterns. Lucas and Sarah honed their instincts, discerning the authentic from the illusory with precision forged from their shared experiences.

Their pursuit through the Mirage demanded a delicate balance—a symbiotic interplay of skepticism and trust, a persistent effort to unravel the layers of deception that veiled the truth. Lucas and Sarah approached each clue with a discerning eye, dismantling the Mirage with a resolute determination to uncover the elusive reality obscured within.

In their pursuit of unraveling the Mirage, Lucas and Sarah leaned on their unity, their collaboration a harmonious synchrony amidst the deceptive choreography that surrounded them. With each fragment decoded, they drew closer to piercing through the enigmatic veil and confronting the truth that had eluded them.

The Mirage's unraveling became a testament to their resilience—a relentless endeavor to dismantle the deceptive illusions and reclaim their grasp on reality. Lucas and Sarah pressed forward, unwavering in their determination to navigate through the mirage and emerge victorious from the echoes of the Puppet Master's manipulative designs.

Chapter 27

Chapter 27: "Mind's Eye Revelation"

Lucas Black and Sarah Martinez stood at the precipice of the Mind's Eye Revelation, a pivotal moment in their relentless pursuit of truth amidst the enigmatic maze of illusions and deception.

The city's labyrinth seemed to pulse with an ethereal energy, the remnants of the Puppet Master's manipulations echoing through its urban expanse. Lucas and Sarah traversed through the streets, their senses heightened, attuned to the subtle nuances that hinted at the revelation lurking within the shadows.

Their investigation room stood as a sanctuary amidst the chaos, adorned with fragments of clues and enigmatic symbols—a testament to their unwavering commitment to unraveling the mysteries that lay shrouded within the Mind's Eye Revelation.

Lucas and Sarah approached each cryptic symbol and elusive clue with meticulous precision, delving deeper into the intricate tapestry of illusions in pursuit of the revelation. Their unity and shared resolve served as a compass, guiding them through the deceptive choreography orchestrated by the Phantom.

As they dissected the fragments of evidence, a sense of anticipation surged—a realization that they stood on the verge of uncovering the truth concealed within the Mind's Eye Revelation. Lucas and Sarah pieced together the enigmatic patterns, their determination unyielding in the face of the complex puzzle before them.

The Mind's Eye Revelation demanded a convergence of instinct and intuition, a synchrony of perception that transcended the boundaries of deception. Lucas and Sarah navigated through the enigmatic maze, honing their senses to discern the authentic from the illusory, drawing upon their shared experiences and mutual trust.

In the heart of their pursuit, the revelation began to materialize—a gradual unveiling of the obscured truth that lay within the labyrinth of illusions. Lucas and Sarah embraced the clarity that emerged, a revelation forged from their resilience and unwavering determination to confront the elusive reality hidden within the Mind's Eye Revelation.

As the fragments coalesced into a cohesive picture, Lucas and Sarah stood on the brink of a profound understanding—a moment where the echoes of the Puppet Master's manipulations dissipated, leaving behind a revelation that pierced through the veils of deception.

The Mind's Eye Revelation was a culmination of their arduous journey—a testament to their relentless pursuit of truth amidst the complexities of manipulation and illusion. Lucas and Sarah stood united, poised to confront the revelation that had eluded them, their unwavering commitment guiding them toward the clarity that awaited within the echoes of the elusive Phantom's enigmatic designs.

Chapter 28

Chapter 28: "Confronting the Manipulator"

Lucas Black and Sarah Martinez, armed with the revelations gleaned from the Mind's Eye Revelation, found themselves on the brink of confronting the Manipulator—the elusive Phantom whose intricate manipulations had woven a web of illusions, entangling their pursuit in a labyrinth of deception.

The city's pulse resonated with an eerie silence as Lucas and Sarah moved through its streets. The remnants of the Puppet Master's manipulations lingered, but their resolve remained steadfast, bolstered by the clarity they had uncovered.

Their investigation room, a bastion of understanding amidst the city's complexities, bore witness to their preparations. Fragments of deciphered clues adorned the walls, forming a mosaic that charted the path to the Manipulator's elusive identity.

Lucas and Sarah synchronized their thoughts, meticulously strategizing their approach as they prepared to confront the Manipulator. Every revelation, every cryptic symbol, and every elusive clue served as ammunition in their pursuit to confront the mastermind behind the labyrinth of manipulation.

Their unity became their strength—a shared determination to confront the Manipulator and unravel the intricacies of the enigmatic web that had ensnared them. Lucas and Sarah braced themselves, knowing that the confrontation ahead would test not only their resilience but also their resolve to face the truth.

As they navigated through the city's streets, anticipation coursed through their veins—a palpable tension that heralded the imminent confrontation. Each step brought them closer to the denouement, to the decisive moment where the Manipulator's elusive guise would be cast aside.

Lucas and Sarah stood at the threshold of the Manipulator's domain, their minds fortified by the revelations gleaned from their arduous journey. With a shared understanding forged from the complexities they had navigated, they prepared to confront the enigmatic figure who had orchestrated the Dance of Deception and woven the Mirage.

Their confrontation with the Manipulator was a testament to their resilience—a culmination of their unwavering pursuit of truth amidst the Puppet Master's manipulative designs. Lucas and Sarah braced themselves, ready to confront the elusive figure and unveil the truth that lay hidden behind the intricate façade of manipulation.

Chapter 29

Chapter 29: "The Veil of Paranoia"

Lucas Black and Sarah Martinez, on the cusp of confronting the Manipulator, found themselves enveloped in the Veil of Paranoia—a pervasive sense of unease as they neared the climax of their pursuit.

The city's atmosphere seemed charged with a palpable tension, echoing the remnants of the Puppet Master's manipulations. Lucas and Sarah navigated the labyrinthine streets cautiously, each step weighed down by a sense of impending confrontation.

Their investigation room, a sanctuary amidst the city's turmoil, bore witness to the Veil of Paranoia. Fragments of decoded clues and enigmatic symbols adorned the walls, a testament to their tireless efforts to pierce through the elusive veil that shrouded the Manipulator's identity.

Lucas and Sarah's shared determination became a beacon of unity amidst the veil of paranoia that clouded their thoughts. Every deciphered clue, every piece of evidence, and every revelation bolstered their resolve as they prepared to confront the elusive figure behind the veil.

The anticipation of the impending confrontation gnawed at their senses, heightening their awareness to the smallest nuances in their surroundings. The echoes of deception lingered, whispering hints of doubt and caution as they moved closer to the climax of their pursuit.

As they approached the rendezvous point where the confrontation was to unfold, the Veil of Paranoia intensified. Lucas and Sarah braced themselves, steeling their nerves against the insidious tendrils of doubt that threatened to cloud their judgment.

Their shared commitment to uncovering the truth served as a shield against the Veil of Paranoia. Lucas and Sarah moved forward with a unified purpose, prepared to confront the manipulative figure and unveil the truth that lay obscured behind the enigmatic façade.

In the heart of the city's enigmatic landscape, Lucas and Sarah stood on the precipice of the confrontation, the Veil of Paranoia a looming presence that tested their fortitude. With resolute determination, they steeled themselves to confront the elusive Manipulator, prepared to cast aside the veil that had veiled their pursuit and reveal the truth that awaited beyond.

Chapter 30

Chapter 30: "Invisible Strings"

Lucas Black and Sarah Martinez found themselves entangled in a web of Invisible Strings, unseen forces that seemed to manipulate the very fabric of their pursuit as they approached the climax of their confrontation with the Manipulator.

The city's streets whispered tales of uncertainty, carrying echoes of the Puppet Master's manipulations that lingered like invisible threads weaving through the urban expanse. Lucas and Sarah moved cautiously, acutely aware of the unseen forces at play.

Their investigation room, a bastion of understanding amidst the complexities, bore witness to the Invisible Strings that entwined their pursuit. Fragments of decoded clues and cryptic symbols adorned the walls, a testament to their perseverance amidst the elusive forces that veiled the truth.

Lucas and Sarah grappled with the intangible nature of the Invisible Strings, recognizing the subtle manipulations that sought to sway their judgment as they prepared to confront the Manipulator. Every revelation, every clue, and every calculated move became a tug-of-war against the unseen forces that clouded their path.

As they approached the anticipated confrontation, the Invisible Strings seemed to intensify, weaving a tapestry of doubt and uncertainty around them. Lucas and Sarah braced themselves, their unity a bulwark against the invisible forces that sought to undermine their resolve.

Their determination remained unyielding—a shared commitment to unraveling the truth obscured by the Invisible Strings. Lucas and Sarah navigated through the invisible maze, their instincts honed to discern the authentic from the illusory, drawing strength from their unwavering partnership.

In the heart of the city's enigmatic labyrinth, Lucas and Sarah stood poised for the decisive confrontation, the Invisible Strings a testament to the manipulative web that surrounded them. With steely determination, they prepared to confront the Manipulator, ready to cast aside the unseen forces and reveal the truth that lay obscured beyond the veils of manipulation.

Chapter 31

Chapter 31: "Deciphering the Code"

Lucas Black and Sarah Martinez, on the threshold of their confrontation with the Manipulator, found themselves immersed in the challenge of Deciphering the Code—a crucial endeavor to unlock the final mysteries that lay concealed within the enigmatic labyrinth of their pursuit.

The city's atmosphere crackled with anticipation, echoing the remnants of the Puppet Master's manipulations. Lucas and Sarah moved with cautious determination, their minds attuned to unraveling the intricate code that veiled the truth.

Their investigation room stood as a testament to their dedication, adorned with fragments of deciphered clues and cryptic symbols—a mosaic of enigmatic patterns that hinted at the underlying truth waiting to be revealed.

Lucas and Sarah meticulously examined every fragment, every symbol, and every elusive clue, piecing together the intricate code that governed the Manipulator's designs. Their unity and shared resolve became a compass, guiding them through the complexities of deciphering the code that held the key to the ultimate revelation.

As they delved deeper into the challenge of deciphering the code, a sense of urgency pervaded their pursuit. The echoes of the Puppet Master's manipulations seemed to intensify, urging them forward as they approached the moment of truth.

Their pursuit through the code demanded a fusion of intellect and intuition, a relentless endeavor to decode the elusive patterns and discern the truth from the labyrinth of manipulation. Lucas and Sarah synchronized their thoughts, drawing upon their shared experiences and mutual trust to unravel the cryptic code that obscured the final revelation.

In the heart of the city's intricate landscape, Lucas and Sarah stood on the precipice of the climactic confrontation, their determination unyielding as they endeavored to decipher the code that held the answers they sought. With unwavering resolve, they prepared to confront the Manipulator armed with the understanding forged from their relentless pursuit and the deciphered code that would unravel the mysteries concealed within the enigmatic labyrinth.

Chapter 32

Chapter 32: "Chasing Ghosts"

Lucas Black and Sarah Martinez, nearing the apex of their confrontation with the Manipulator, found themselves ensnared in the paradox of Chasing Ghosts—a haunting pursuit of elusive figures and fleeting truths that danced at the periphery of their investigation.

The city's ambiance held an eerie resonance, echoing the remnants of the Puppet Master's manipulations. Lucas and Sarah moved through the urban landscape with a sense of urgency, chasing elusive echoes and fleeting apparitions that seemed to dissolve upon their approach.

Their investigation room, a sanctuary amidst the city's complexities, bore witness to their relentless pursuit of elusive figures and ephemeral clues. Fragments of decoded messages and cryptic symbols adorned the walls—a testament to their persistent chase of the intangible phantoms that led them closer to the Manipulator.

Lucas and Sarah grappled with the enigmatic nature of Chasing Ghosts, recognizing that every elusive figure they pursued held a fragment of truth. Every fleeting encounter, every ephemeral apparition became a clue in their relentless pursuit, a puzzle piece in the intricate mosaic they sought to unravel.

As they delved deeper into the chase, the echoes of the Puppet Master's manipulations seemed to taunt them, leading them down elusive trails that dissipated into uncertainty. Lucas and Sarah pressed forward, driven by an unyielding determination to grasp the fleeting truths that lingered within the echoes of their pursuit.

Their pursuit through the maze of Chasing Ghosts demanded resilience—a tenacious effort to seize elusive glimpses of reality from the ethereal shadows that haunted their investigation. Lucas and Sarah forged ahead, drawing upon their unity and shared resolve to chase down the elusive phantoms and unravel the truths they concealed.

In the heart of the city's enigmatic landscape, Lucas and Sarah stood on the precipice of their confrontation, their pursuit of the elusive figures a testament to their unwavering resolve. With determination forged from their relentless chase, they prepared to confront the Manipulator, armed not only with the deciphered clues but also with the fleeting truths gleaned from their haunting pursuit of elusive apparitions.

Chapter 33

Chapter 33: "Betrayal's Shattered Mirrors"

Lucas Black and Sarah Martinez found themselves entangled in the disarray of Betrayal's Shattered Mirrors—a haunting realization that the reflections of trust had been fractured, leaving behind shards of deception in their pursuit of the Manipulator.

The city's atmosphere was fraught with tension, echoes of the Puppet Master's manipulations lingering as fractured reflections in the shattered mirrors of trust. Lucas and Sarah moved cautiously, navigating the remnants of their fractured trust, wary of further deceit.

Their investigation room stood as a testament to the broken mirrors of betrayal. Fragments of deciphered clues and cryptic symbols adorned the walls, a fragmented mosaic that mirrored the shattered trust they grappled with.

Lucas and Sarah confronted the disarray of Betrayal's Shattered Mirrors, the realization of deception weaving an intricate tapestry of doubt. Every shattered fragment, every broken reflection served as a stark reminder of the trust that had been fractured by the Manipulator's machinations.

As they traversed the city's intricate landscape, the shattered mirrors of betrayal seemed to cast distorted reflections of their journey, distorting their perceptions and clouding their judgment. Lucas and Sarah navigated through the fragmented trust with caution, their unity serving as a beacon amidst the fractured echoes of deception.

Their pursuit through Betrayal's Shattered Mirrors demanded resilience—a relentless effort to piece together the shattered fragments of trust and discern the truth amidst the distorted reflections. Lucas and Sarah forged ahead, drawing upon their shared resolve to confront the Manipulator while navigating through the remnants of their fractured trust.

In the heart of the city's tumultuous landscape, Lucas and Sarah stood poised for the final confrontation, their determination unyielding despite the fractured mirrors of betrayal. With a determination forged from their enduring partnership, they prepared to confront the Manipulator, armed not only with the deciphered clues but also with the insights gleaned from the shattered reflections of trust that adorned their arduous pursuit.

Chapter 34

Chapter 34: "The Mental Maze"

Lucas Black and Sarah Martinez found themselves ensnared in the intricate complexities of The Mental Maze—a labyrinthine construct of the mind that obscured the path to truth and clarity as they neared the climax of their pursuit.

The city's ambiance resonated with an enigmatic aura, echoing the remnants of the Puppet Master's manipulations. Lucas and Sarah moved cautiously, their thoughts entangled within the intricate pathways of the mental maze, navigating through the convoluted corridors of perception and deceit.

Their investigation room stood as a bastion amidst the mental maze, adorned with fragments of deciphered clues and cryptic symbols—a testament to their tireless efforts to unravel the complexities that veiled the truth.

Lucas and Sarah grappled with the perplexing nature of The Mental Maze, recognizing that every turn led to a convolution of thoughts and perceptions. Each step forward became a calculated maneuver, a deliberate attempt to navigate through the intricate corridors of their minds and discern the genuine from the illusory.

As they delved deeper into the mental maze, the echoes of the Puppet Master's manipulations seemed to reverberate louder, clouding their judgment and weaving a complex tapestry of uncertainty. Lucas and Sarah pressed on, their unity serving as a compass amidst the labyrinthine complexities of their thoughts.

Their pursuit through The Mental Maze demanded resilience—a tireless effort to unravel the tangled threads of perception and deceit that clouded their understanding. Lucas and Sarah persisted, drawing upon their shared resolve to confront the Manipulator while navigating through the convoluted pathways of their minds.

In the heart of the city's enigmatic landscape, Lucas and Sarah stood on the threshold of the final confrontation, their determination unyielding despite the perplexing nature of The Mental Maze. With a resolute spirit forged from their unwavering partnership, they prepared to confront the Manipulator, armed not only with the deciphered clues but also with the insights gleaned from the intricate corridors of their intertwined thoughts.

Chapter 35

Chapter 35: "Unmasking the Phantom"

Lucas Black and Sarah Martinez stood at the culmination of their arduous journey, poised on the brink of Unmasking the Phantom—the pivotal moment where the elusive Manipulator's identity would be revealed, and the truth laid bare.

The city's atmosphere hummed with anticipation, echoes of the Puppet Master's manipulations lingering as a haunting reminder of their relentless pursuit. Lucas and Sarah moved with a sense of purpose, their steps guided by an unyielding determination to uncover the truth concealed behind the elusive façade.

Their investigation room served as the nexus of their final preparations, adorned with fragments of deciphered clues and cryptic symbols—a mosaic of evidence that pointed towards the revelation of the Phantom's identity.

Lucas and Sarah confronted the climax of their pursuit with unwavering resolve, their unity an anchor amidst the uncertainties that loomed before them. Each piece of evidence, every cryptic message, and all the intricate threads of deception they had unraveled led them closer to the moment of unmasking the elusive Manipulator.

As they approached the final confrontation, the echoes of the Puppet Master's manipulations seemed to intensify, a last attempt to cloak the Phantom's identity in shadows of doubt. Lucas and Sarah pushed forward, their shared determination a shield against the veils of deception that sought to obscure the truth.

Their pursuit to unmask the Phantom demanded unwavering perseverance—a culmination of their relentless efforts to unravel the enigmatic web that had ensnared them. Lucas and Sarah stood resolute, prepared to confront the elusive figure behind the intricate manipulations that had woven a tapestry of deception.

In the heart of the city's suspenseful landscape, Lucas and Sarah readied themselves for the final encounter, their determination unshakeable despite the lingering echoes of the Phantom's manipulative designs. With steadfast determination forged from their enduring partnership, they braced themselves to unmask the elusive Manipulator, ready to unveil the truth that had eluded them throughout their perilous journey.

Chapter 36

Chapter 36: "The Illusion of Truth"

Lucas Black and Sarah Martinez found themselves entangled in the intricate web of The Illusion of Truth—a paradoxical realm where reality blurred and the elusive nature of truth was shrouded in deceptive veils.

The city's atmosphere seemed to echo with enigmatic whispers, remnants of the Puppet Master's manipulations lingering as deceptive mirages. Lucas and Sarah moved cautiously, navigating through the distorted landscape where truth seemed to intertwine with illusion.

Their investigation room stood as a sanctuary amidst the illusions, adorned with fragments of deciphered clues and cryptic symbols—a testament to their tireless pursuit of the elusive truth that danced on the edges of perception.

Lucas and Sarah grappled with the complexities of The Illusion of Truth, recognizing that every glimpse of clarity was shadowed by layers of deception. The elusive nature of their pursuit demanded a meticulous dissection of reality from the deceptive illusions that clouded their judgment.

As they delved deeper into the illusionary realm, the echoes of the Puppet Master's manipulations seemed to intensify, weaving a tapestry of uncertainty that obscured the truth they sought. Lucas and Sarah pressed on, their unity a guiding light amidst the deceptive shadows that surrounded them.

Their pursuit through The Illusion of Truth demanded unwavering resolve—a persistent effort to untangle the enigmatic threads that blurred reality and illusion. Lucas and Sarah forged ahead, drawing upon their shared determination to confront the Manipulator while discerning the genuine from the illusory.

In the heart of the city's perplexing landscape, Lucas and Sarah stood poised on the brink of the final revelation, their determination unyielding despite the elusive nature of The Illusion of Truth. With steadfast resolve forged from their unwavering partnership, they prepared to confront the Manipulator, armed not only with the deciphered clues but also with the insights gleaned from navigating the deceptive maze of illusion and reality.

Chapter 37

Chapter 37: "Battle of Wits"

Lucas Black and Sarah Martinez stood on the verge of the Battle of Wits—a decisive confrontation with the elusive Manipulator that would test their intellect, resilience, and strategic acumen in a battle for truth and justice.

The city's atmosphere crackled with anticipation, echoes of the Puppet Master's manipulations lingering as a testament to the challenge that lay ahead. Lucas and Sarah moved with a calculated determination, preparing for the mental duel that awaited them.

Their investigation room served as a battleground of intellect, adorned with fragments of decoded clues and cryptic symbols—a tableau of evidence that represented the culmination of their tireless pursuit of truth.

Lucas and Sarah prepared themselves for the Battle of Wits, recognizing that every move, every decision, and every deduction would shape the outcome of their confrontation with the elusive Manipulator. They honed their mental prowess, anticipating the strategic complexities that would unfold in the impending showdown.

As they approached the final confrontation, the echoes of the Puppet Master's manipulations seemed to heighten, a reminder of the intricate battle that lay before them. Lucas and Sarah fortified themselves, their unity a pillar of strength in the face of the manipulative intricacies that surrounded them.

Their pursuit in the Battle of Wits demanded unwavering vigilance—a test of their astuteness and ingenuity in unraveling the elaborate machinations of their adversary. Lucas and Sarah advanced with determination, ready to engage in a cerebral duel to expose the truth and triumph over the elusive Manipulator.

In the heart of the city's anticipatory atmosphere, Lucas and Sarah readied themselves for the mental face-off, their determination resolute despite the challenging complexities of the Battle of Wits. With a steadfast resolve forged from their enduring partnership, they prepared to confront the Manipulator, armed not only with the deciphered clues but also with the strategic prowess that would define the outcome of their cerebral confrontation.

Chapter 38

Chapter 38: "The Mind's Abyss"

Lucas Black and Sarah Martinez found themselves teetering on the edge of The Mind's Abyss—an unfathomable chasm where the depths of the human psyche intertwined with the enigmatic complexities of their pursuit, leading them closer to the elusive Manipulator.

The city's ambiance echoed with an eerie resonance, remnants of the Puppet Master's manipulations haunting their thoughts. Lucas and Sarah navigated cautiously, on the precipice of an unknown abyss within their own minds, where truth and deception intertwined in a labyrinth of complexities.

Their investigation room became a realm of introspection amidst the city's turmoil, adorned with fragments of deciphered clues and cryptic symbols—a testament to their journey into the depths of their own perceptions and the Manipulator's design.

Lucas and Sarah grappled with the daunting depths of The Mind's Abyss, recognizing that every step forward plunged them into the intricacies of their own thoughts and perceptions. The psychological complexity of their pursuit demanded a profound introspection, a navigation through the recesses of their minds.

As they delved deeper into The Mind's Abyss, the echoes of the Puppet Master's manipulations resonated louder, whispering uncertainties and doubts that echoed within their minds. Lucas and Sarah persisted, their unity a guiding light amidst the psychological shadows that enveloped them.

Their pursuit through The Mind's Abyss demanded unwavering self-awareness—a journey into the depths of their own psyche to untangle the intricate web of thoughts and emotions. Lucas and Sarah forged ahead, drawing upon their shared resolve to confront the Manipulator while navigating through the psychological labyrinth.

In the heart of the city's introspective landscape, Lucas and Sarah stood on the threshold of self-discovery, their determination unyielding despite the profound complexities of The Mind's Abyss. With unwavering determination forged from their enduring partnership, they prepared to confront the Manipulator, armed not only with the deciphered clues but also with the profound insights gleaned from their introspective journey into the depths of their own minds.

Chapter 39

Chapter 39: "Shattered Illusions"

Lucas Black and Sarah Martinez confronted the aftermath of Shattered Illusions—a pivotal moment where the deceptive facade began to crumble, revealing the stark truth hidden behind the veils of manipulation and deceit.

The city's atmosphere carried a sense of upheaval, echoes of the Puppet Master's manipulations fading as the truth began to emerge. Lucas and Sarah moved with a cautious determination, navigating through the remnants of shattered illusions that once clouded their pursuit.

Their investigation room stood as a testament to the shattered illusions, fragments of decoded clues and cryptic symbols adorning the walls—a mosaic of evidence that depicted the disintegration of the deceptive facades they had encountered.

Lucas and Sarah grappled with the revelations brought forth by the shattered illusions, recognizing that every fractured facade led them closer to the raw truth. The dissolution of deceit demanded a recalibration of their understanding and an acceptance of the reality that emerged from the debris of illusions.

As they navigated through the aftermath of Shattered Illusions, the echoes of the Puppet Master's manipulations gradually dissipated, revealing glimpses of clarity amid the fragmented remnants. Lucas and Sarah pressed forward, their unity a stabilizing force amidst the dissolution of deceptive facades.

Their pursuit through the aftermath of Shattered Illusions demanded adaptability—a resilience to accept the unveiling truth amid the shattered remnants of deception. Lucas and Sarah forged ahead, drawing upon their shared resolve to confront the reality that emerged from the dissolving illusions.

In the heart of the city's transitional landscape, Lucas and Sarah stood poised on the verge of clarity, their determination unyielding despite the unsettling aftermath of Shattered Illusions. With unwavering resolve forged from their enduring partnership, they prepared to confront the Manipulator, armed not only with the deciphered clues but also with the acceptance and understanding that arose from the shattered remnants of illusions.

Chapter 40

Chapter 40: "The Final Mind Game"

Lucas Black and Sarah Martinez stood on the precipice of The Final Mind Game—a decisive encounter that marked the culmination of their relentless pursuit, pitting their intellect and resilience against the elusive Manipulator in a battle for truth and resolution.

The city's atmosphere crackled with tension, remnants of the Puppet Master's manipulations fading into the backdrop. Lucas and Sarah moved with a calculated determination, bracing themselves for the ultimate mental challenge that lay ahead.

Their investigation room served as the arena for The Final Mind Game, adorned with fragments of deciphered clues and cryptic symbols—a testament to their unyielding determination to unravel the elusive Manipulator's designs.

Lucas and Sarah confronted the final challenge with unwavering resolve, recognizing that every move, every deduction, and every decision would shape the outcome of their ultimate confrontation. They prepared themselves mentally, sharpening their intellect for the impending showdown.

As they approached the decisive encounter, the echoes of the Puppet Master's manipulations dissipated, paving the way for a clear path ahead. Lucas and Sarah fortified themselves, their unity a source of strength amid the mental challenges that lay ahead.

Their pursuit through The Final Mind Game demanded unwavering focus—a culmination of their mental acumen and strategic planning in a battle that transcended mere intellect. Lucas and Sarah advanced with determination, ready to engage in a cerebral duel to expose the truth and bring resolution to their arduous journey.

In the heart of the city's charged atmosphere, Lucas and Sarah readied themselves for the ultimate mental face-off, their determination resolute despite the weight of the final challenge. With steadfast resolve forged from their enduring partnership, they prepared to confront the Manipulator, armed not only with the deciphered clues but also with the unwavering determination to triumph in The Final Mind Game and unravel the truth that had eluded them throughout their perilous pursuit.

Milton Keynes UK
Ingram Content Group UK Ltd.
UKHW012137010124
435322UK00003B/61